BARBAPAPA

Annette Tison and Talus Taylor

ORCHARD

Barbapapa was born in a garden.

Barbazoo

Barbabright

Barbabeau

Barbalala

ORCHARD BOOKS
338 Euston Road, London NW1 3BH
Orchard Books Australia
Level 17/207 Kent Street, Sydney, NSW 2000
First published in 1970
This edition published in the UK by Orchard Books 2013
ISBN 9781408330715

A CIP catalogue record for this book is available from the British Library.
1 3 5 7 9 10 8 6 4 2
Printed in Italy
Orchard Books is a division of Hachette Children's Books, an Hachette UK company.
www.hachette.co.uk

That day, François was watering the flowers.

François' mother said that Barbapapa was too big to stay with them.

Barbapapa had to go to the zoo.

He was unhappy because he had to live in a cage.

Barbapapa found he could change his shape and so he escaped.

He wanted to play with the other animals.

He tried to make friends . . .

. . . but they didn’t understand.

The director of the zoo was very angry because Barbapapa had left his cage . . .

. . . and he ordered Barbapapa to leave the zoo forever.

Barbapapa wandered into the city but the cars frightened him.

There was nowhere he could go.

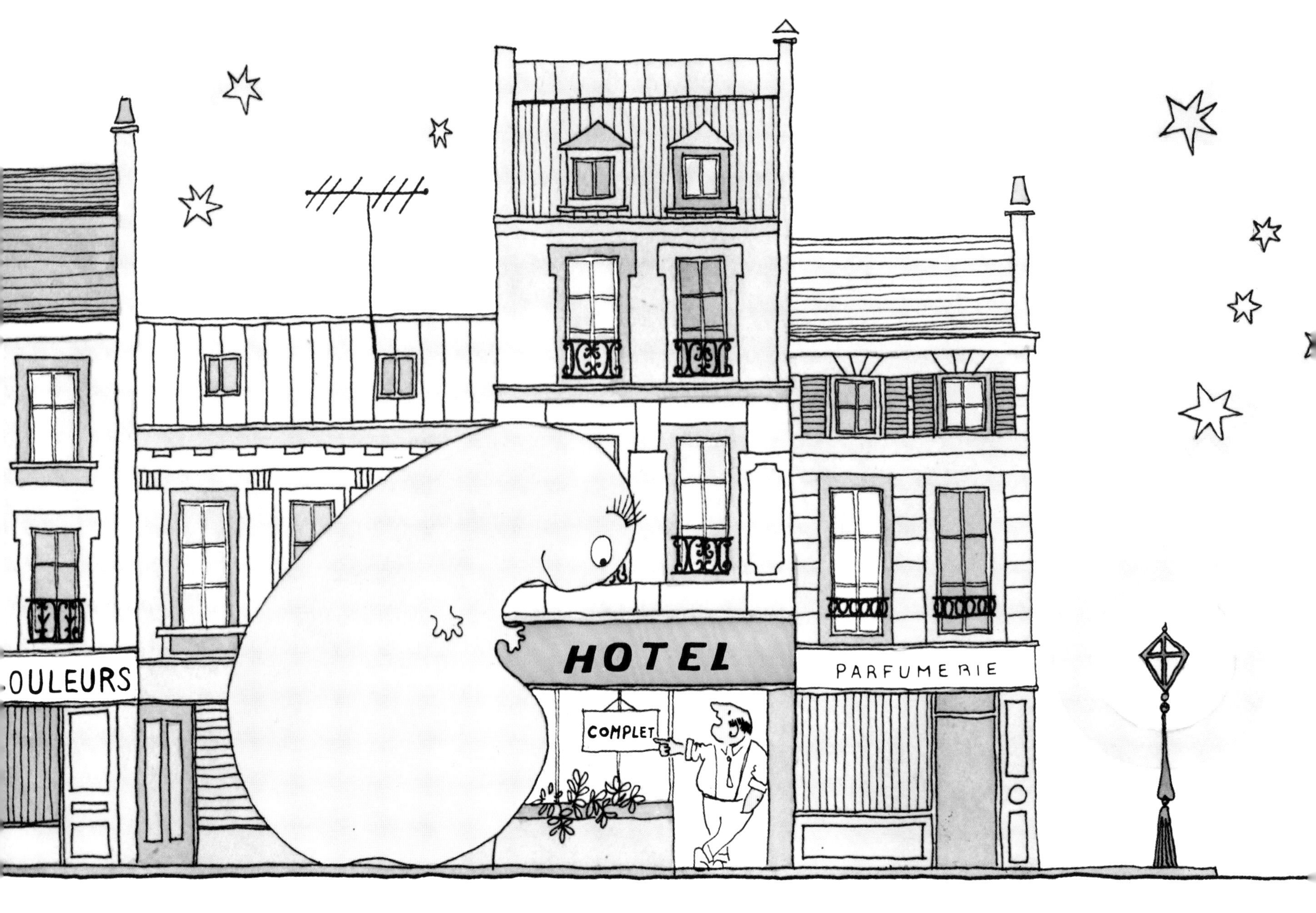

He had no money and no friends.

Barbapapa was all alone and he cried. But look! A fire!

Barbapapa came to the rescue.

The firemen were grateful for his help.

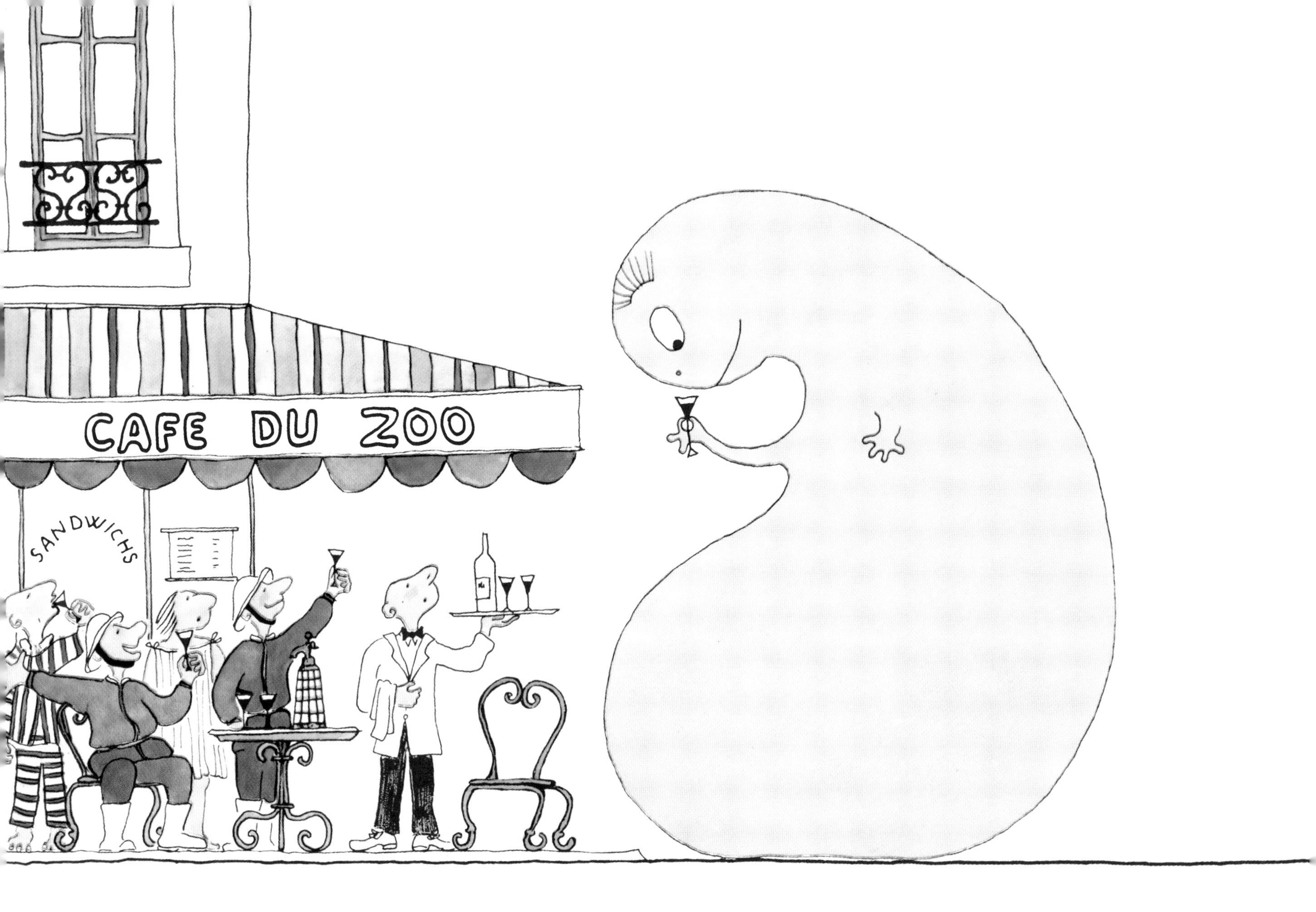

While they were having a party after the fire, Barbapapa heard cries for help.

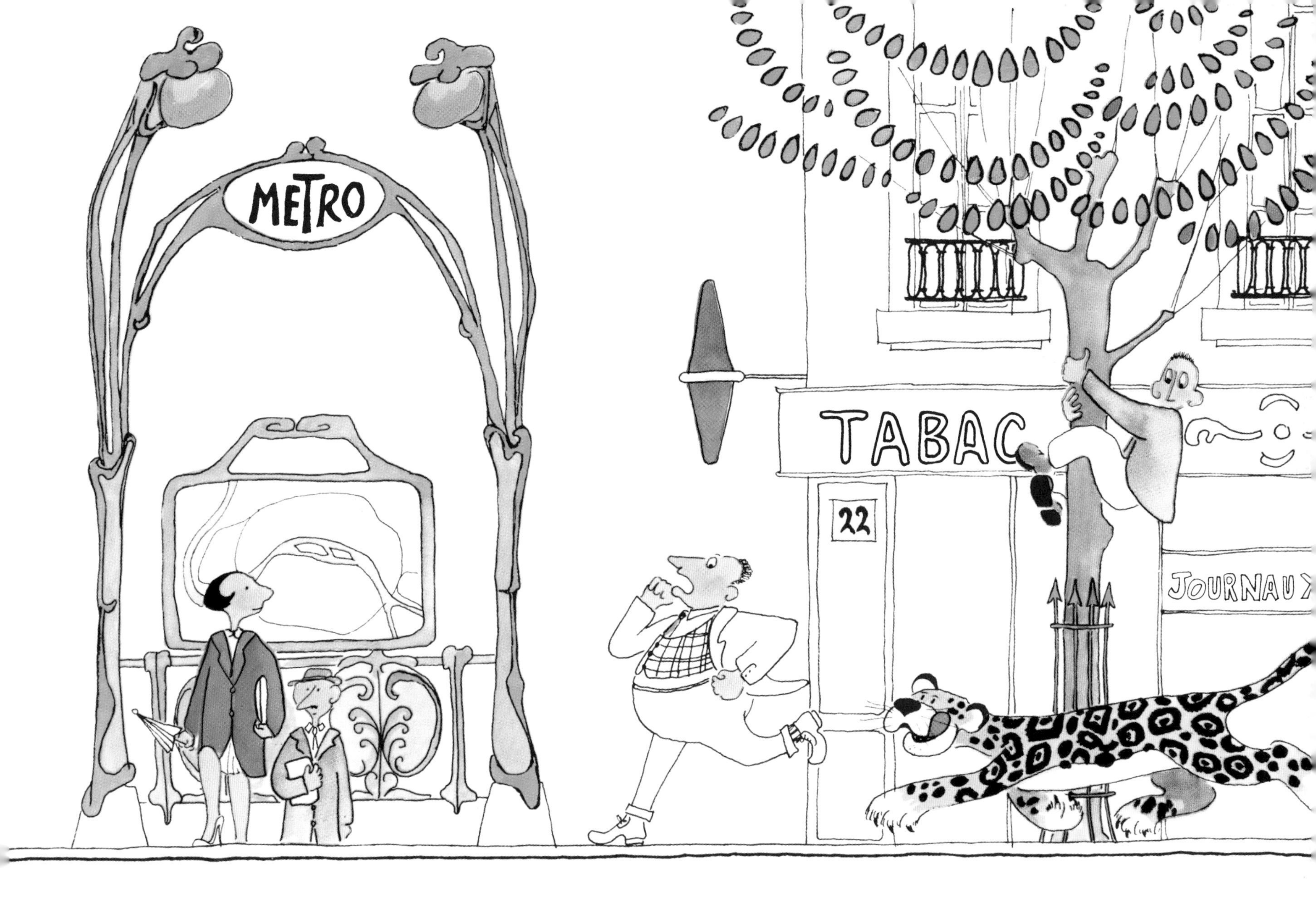

A fierce leopard had escaped from the zoo.

Barbapapa caught him quite easily.

The leopard was returned to the zoo in time for dinner.

Barbapapa became famous.

The city gave him a hero's welcome.

Barbapapa came back to live with François.

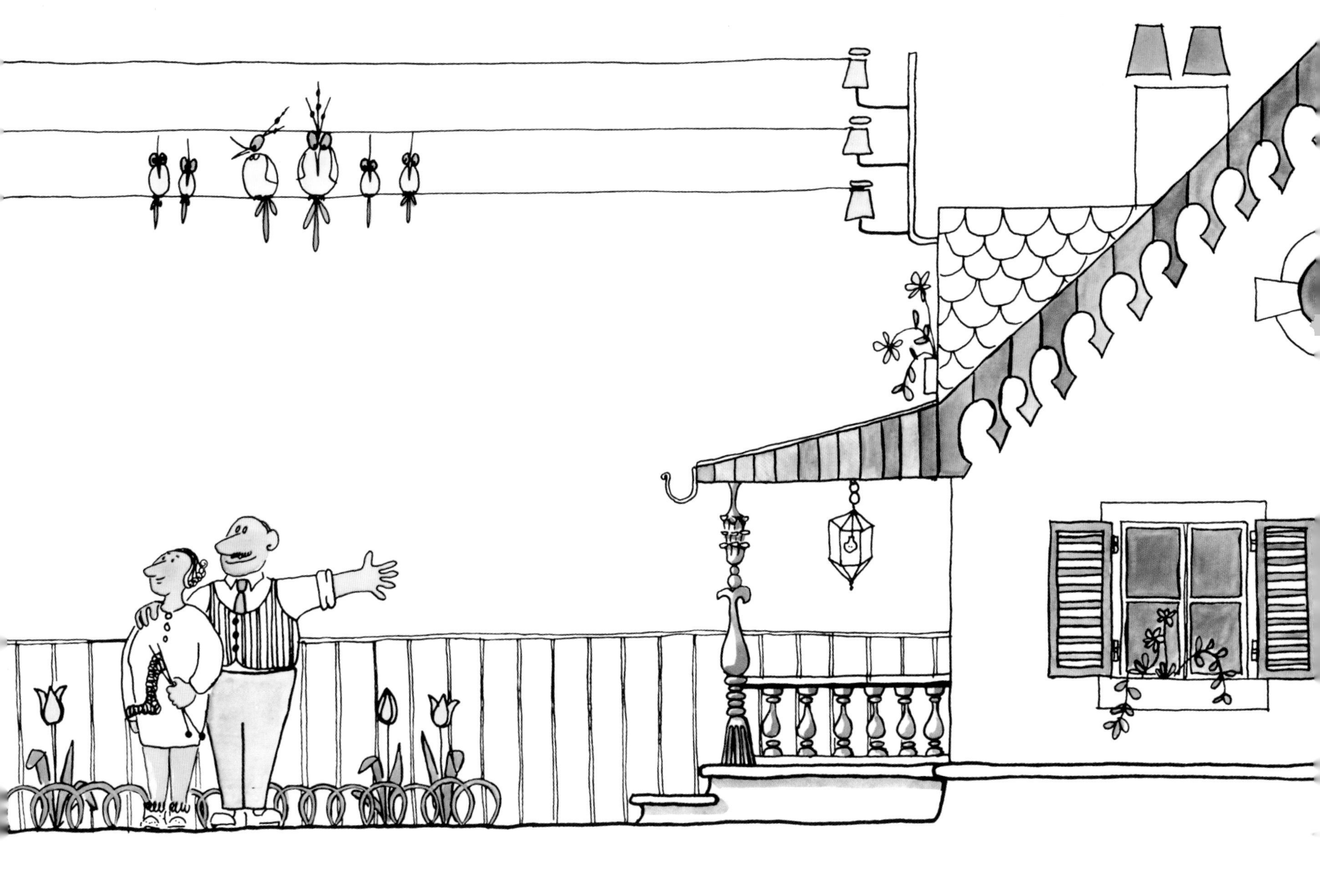

François' parents were delighted.

François' father built a house for Barbapapa.

Barbapapa played with the children.

Sometimes Barbapapa met his friends in the park . . .

. . . and everyone was happy to see him.

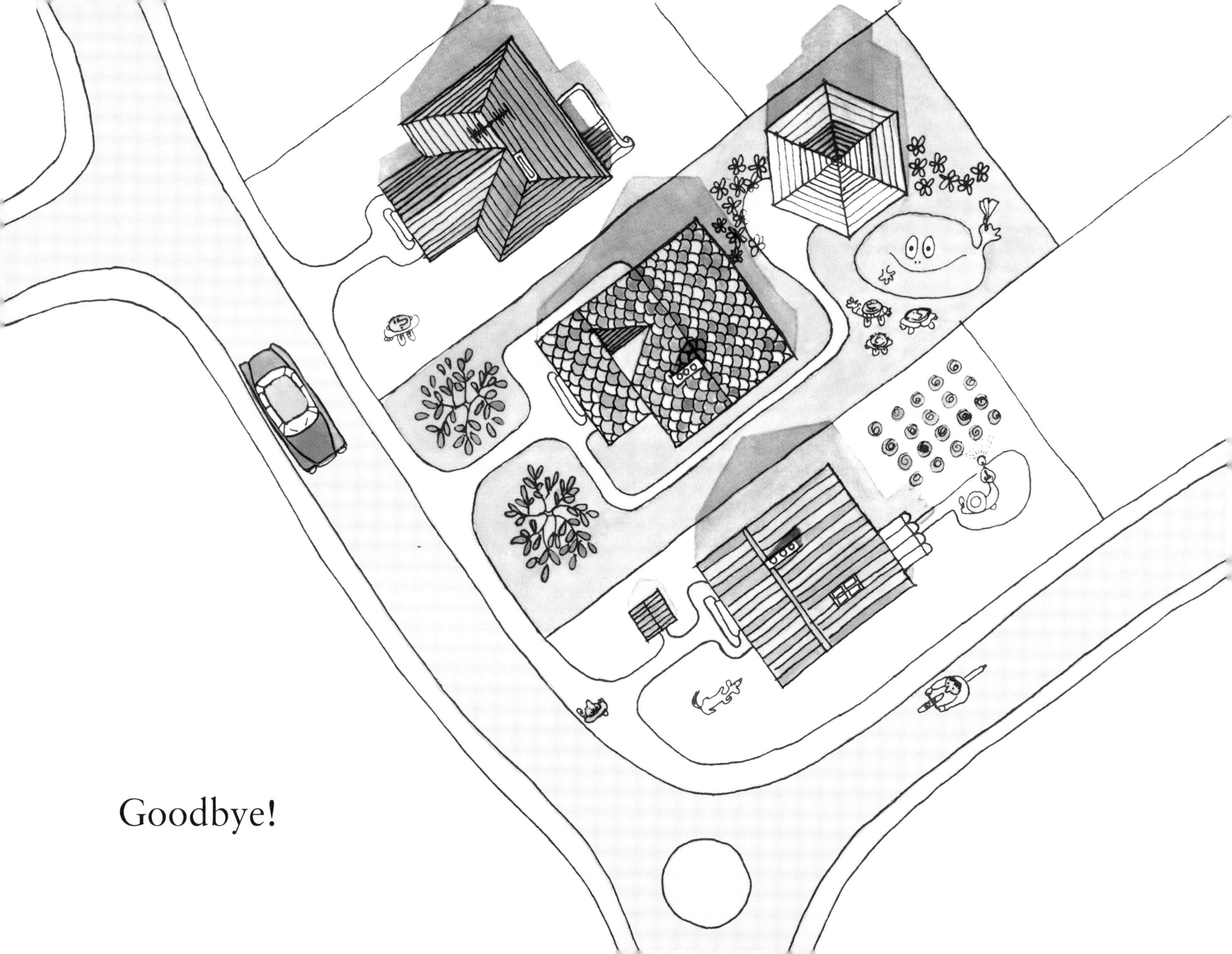

Goodbye!

Barbabravo

Barbabella

Barbalib